GOING THROUGH HELL

BY

KYMBER JONES

ISBN

Published in India 2021 by Pencil

A brand of
One Point Six Technologies Pvt. Ltd.
123, Building J2, Shram Seva Premises,
Wadala Truck Terminal, Wadala (E)
Mumbai 400037, Maharashtra, INDIA
E connect@thepencilapp.com
W www.thepencilapp.com

AUTHOR BIOGRAPHY

Kymber Jones is the name, Kym Jones is using for her adult book, and Going Through Hell is her first 18+ novella. She spent 12 years in the Navy getting into more trouble by trying to write (or read) more often than trying to do her job much to the frustration of her superior officers. They let her know when she made it famous, however, to remember them and put them in her books. Which did they mean though, dead or alive (DOA), LoL?

CONTENTS

CHAPTER 1

The Cunt's back. Of course, it's not like she went where she told the Bitch where she was going. She never does. And yet the Bitch keeps letting it happen. Well, we'll see how much longer this goes on. The cunt's going to pay. And she's going to deliver real fucking soon; her and all her friends.

"I fucking hate you!" Rebecca screamed at the top of her lungs as she lunged at Jasmine for what seemed like the hundredth time that hour. "Why can't you just fucking die?!" Rebecca continued with her tirade.

"Why can't you just drop dead?" Jasmine asked her sister. "It's not like you aren't killing yourself already. What with being a drugged-out whore and all."

With an even louder scream, Rebecca threw herself at Jasmine and started pulling her hair as hard as she could.

"All right," a drunk voice said, entering the small, rundown three-bedroom trailer. "Cat-fight. Now take a breather so I can get a beer."

When neither girl listened to the drunken suggestion of pausing their fight, Charles, or Chuck as the girls liked to call him, walked back over to them and grabbed the two of them by their hair, yanking the contestants away from each other as hard as he could.

"Goddammit, I said, stop! Now, are you going to take a fucking breather, or do I have to make you?" Charles demanded.

"Fuck you!" Rebecca turned her venom onto a new target, drawing Charles's daily drunken rage onto herself, allowing Jasmine to untangle her hair from her father's grasp and slink quickly away to the bedroom she shares with Rebecca and lock the door.

Less than a minute later, a soft knock sounded on the door.

"What?!" Jasmine cried, not wanting anyone to bother her.

"Jazz, it's me. I brought you some ice for your face and head." Marla said softly. "Can I come in?"

Jasmine, or Jazz as her family and friends call her, replied, "I guess," as she unlocked the door even though she refused to open it.

Holding out the two baggies of ice wrapped in face clothes, Marla said, "Here you go. Hopefully, you were winning the fight before Chuck stepped in and broke it up."

Jazz glared at Marla for a second, then said, "If you'd been there, you would have seen the result. Where were you? I could have used your help."

"I just got in. I heard Chuck as I entered the kitchen. I have to stay late at school three days a week starting this week, for six weeks, remember?" Marla asked. "I failed math. I'm going to that new mandatory tutoring class with the Principle. God, whoever thought the School Principle was a Math Teacher?! I mean, really! Talk about a nightmare."

Jazz smirked. "Whatever. At least he's cute."

"True. But we can't get away with shit in there."

That caused Jazz to laugh, then immediately broke it off, all the while trying to keep it quiet. "Like you would even try to get away with anything Miss Goody Two Shoes. Have you ever attempted to do something against the rules?"

"I stole a couple of things when I was younger," Marla said, her tone of voice a bit hurt.

Jazz laughed this time, not caring if anyone did hear. "I'm not talking about an accident while at the register and taking it back later to pay for it."

Embarrassment colored Marla's cheek because that was precisely what had happened. Still, she didn't want to admit it or have it gotten out to everyone that she never did anything to get in trouble, especially at school. That would make her already shit life that much worse, but judging by the glint in Jazz's eyes, she knew that's exactly what was about to be happening.

"Hell, if you were family," Jazz said, refusing to acknowledge how Marla's father had married her mother then died less than a week after their marriage took place. Ann, or Annie to those close to her, kept Marla with her because she had nowhere else to go, but everyone made it clear she is not part of the family. Though Ann did try, upon occasion, to make her feel wanted. Or should she say, Annie tried when the mood struck her every couple of decades or so – or in her case, never. When the Anniversary of her father's car accident came, and everyone went to his grave, Annie would have Marla choose one of her favorite meals for dinner and then cook something completely different. She would even get her a card that said something about condolences to try and make herself feel like the mother of the year. "You would have a Juvie record and then some already."

"But then I'm not family, right?" Marla asked.

Jazz looked upset. "What, you think you're too good to call us family?" Jazz demanded.

Marla shook her head. "Not at all. You keep telling me that repeatedly."

"Don't you know a fucking joke when you hear one?" Jazz demanded.

Marla shrugged. "I guess not." She mumbled.

"Sheesh. No wonder your friends call you Prissy.

Everything must be perfect for you. No jokes or anything. You're never going to have a boyfriend this way."

"Well, right now, I don't even want a boyfriend, so I don't care," Marla said.

All Jazz did is roll her eyes and say, "Okay," all drawn out, causing Marla to sigh.

"Look, all I want to do is focus on school and graduate. And hopefully, get good enough grades to get a scholarship out of here – or at least accepted. But I can't do that with the grades I have right now in math and science, so I must focus on those classes right now. At least science isn't a mandatory study class like math is right now."

"And where would you go? Huh? You don't have any money to go anywhere else. What do you plan on doing? You know damn well, Chuck ain't going to let you waltz your sweet ass into college when you could be working to make him money so he could go out and drink with his friends."

"I just turned sixteen. I only have two more years in this house. Then I'm free to find somewhere else if I have a job."

"Yeah, okay. Like Chuck and Mom would let you leave. Are you kidding? They're not going to let any of us leave. Not unless we can find someone they can mold into their liking."

Marla shuddered. Just the thought of winding up with someone like either Chuck or Annie, though especially Chuck, was enough to make her want to gag. She was going to get out of this nightmare by the time she was in college. And there was no way in hell she was going to end up with a piece of shit like Mr. Up Chuck.

CHAPTER 2

The lying two-faced Spawn from Hell thinks she's so fucking brilliant. She doesn't know I read her diary or that I'm the one who told her current loser she's still seeing her last asshole boyfriend. Nor is she aware I'm the one who informed the last Prick she aborted his son. Not that the bitch did, but that's what I told him. When she came inside the trailer, all black and blue, with just the right hint of purple, I about pissed my pants, trying to keep from laughing.

God, it felt so good to see her get some of what she deserves.

Walking outside of her math class, Marla saw Rebecca leaning against the lockers with Chad, her newest boy toy, and flinched. If Rebecca was waiting, it only meant one thing: Trouble.

Trying not to let Rebecca see how much she got to her, Marla straightened her shoulders and pulled her books closer to her chest. For some reason, just that motion made her feel safer, though why she couldn't begin to say.

When Rebecca saw Marla, she pushed Chad away a bit roughly and stepped closer to her, smirking.

"You hear about Bitch Face yet?" Rebecca asked, her face alight with laughter.

"Which one? You have so many Bitch Faces." Marla said, not wanting to get in the middle of anything with Rebecca, especially at the school.

Don't be a smart ass with me. We both know you won't win," Rebecca said snidely. "The only one that matters right now: Jizz since that's what she's so full of right now. Or do I need to describe what that is to you, along with everything else?"

Marla quickly shook her head no. No way did she want Rebecca teaching her, or showing her, how to do anything! Not if she could help it!

"Look at you! All scared and everything!" Rebecca continued to laugh. "Damn, maybe I should do something, just to see what you do."

"I would rather you didn't," Marla replied, beginning to look anywhere but at Rebecca. For when she was in this mood, there was no telling what she would do next, and Marla didn't want to stick around to find out.

"Okay, okay, fine!" Rebecca yelled, seeing Marla was about to be gone. "Don't get your panties in a bunch. Miz Jizz, the oh-so-perfect lying, two-faced bitch, had the shit knocked out of her this morning. It looks like she met the wrong end of a baseball bat or something."

Marla looked at Rebecca in shock. "Someone beat Jazz?!" She demanded.

Rebecca shrugged. "So?"

"So, she's your sister! You should at least find out how she's doing and if she needs help!"

"It's not like I care." Rebecca glared at Marla. "Why would I ask if she needs help?"

"Because she's your sister, and that's what family does."

"Yeah, right. And you would, you know? It's not like you have any family."

"I have family somewhere." Marla retorted.

Rebecca snorted. "Yeah, right. If your sorry ass had any family left, they sure as hell don't want anything to do with you, which is why you're still mooching off our family, and that means your family is a lot smarter than you for dumping your sorry stupid ass."

Before she could help it, tears welled up in her eyes and started to leak down the side of Marla's face before Rebecca turned away to focus on the next item of interest.

"Oh, is the baby going to cry?" Rebecca taunted.

Marla quickly wiped her tears away without saying a word of distress.

"Not at all." She replied. "You can say whatever you want. I don't give a flying fuck. All you are is a lying douchebag. So, if you don't mind, I need to go and check on your sister and see how she's doing: see if she's okay."

"Good luck with that. The bitch was sent home for causing a fight in the cafeteria. She'll be black and blue for days by the time Chuck is through with her."

"What did you do to start the fight?" Marla demanded.

"Me?!" Rebecca protested. "What the hell makes you think I did anything? I wasn't even there."

"No, you just told someone some damn lie and let it go from there. You forget I know you. And I know the fucked-up bullshit games you like to play. So, I'm guessing you told some girl a sob story about how Jazz stabbed them in the back, and she turned around and beat Jazz as revenge for you. I wonder how many teachers would be interested in hearing how the events played out."

Rebecca lunged at Marla, grabbing hold of her hair, startling her, but not scaring her as severely as she would have hoped.

"If you ever breathe that shit to anyone, I will make you pay, do you understand me?" Rebecca snarled as she yanked Marla's head as far back as she possibly could.

"Go for it." Marla wheezed. "It won't be anything new."

"Just wait. Once we get home, you'll be wishing you were never born. That's a fucking promise."

As Rebecca yanked on Marla's hair a second time, a teacher turned the corner and watched as Rebecca assaulted her sister.

"Hey!" He shouted. "Miss Petermeire! What do you think you're doing?! Let your sister go right now!"

Rebecca glared at the Teacher, sneering. "And who's going to make me? You? You're barely old enough to shave, let alone teach any of us. And you think you can punish me?"

"I suggest you let Miss Petermeire go, or you're going to be finding out just what I'm capable of doing."

Rebecca laughed. "Yeah, right," she scoffed.

Before Rebecca could say anything else, the Teacher quickly reached up and grabbed her hands, squeezing them roughly to make her release her hold on Marla, then spun her around and held her arms behind her back, shoving her down against the floor.

"Ow! You fucking son of a bitch!" Rebecca screamed. "Let me go! You're hurting me!"

"I don't think so. The only place you're going is with Security as soon as they arrive."'

"I said fucking let me go! I'm going to be telling everyone you fucking sexually assaulted me! Who do you think they're going to believe, huh? Some Goddamn male perv that likes to feel up young women or the young female student he assaulted?"

The Teacher just laughed as he stood up rather quickly, surprising Rebecca.

"I rather hope you do try and claim I assaulted you. That would make this show even more interesting. Now, Oscar's here, and he's just itching to take you into the Security Office. The Principal will be meeting you there. You can tell him all about how I assaulted you."

Passing Rebecca over to the head of Security, the Teacher said, "Here, Brother. Be careful of this one. She bites."

"Just so long as her bites aren't poisonous, then we're all good. Miss. Petermeire, you doing okay?" Oscar asked Marla, his concern for her evident in his voice.

Marla nodded. "I'm fine; thank you." She said. "It's nothing new. I should be going, I can't afford to be late for my next class, and the bell already rang."

"I'll walk you to your class. Your Teacher wouldn't say anything if you were helping me."

Marla looked a little surprised. "Thank you, I guess." She told the Teacher. "But why are you doing this? I'm not one of your students."

As Marla and the Teacher who interfered on her behalf began walking to her class, she looked up at him and waited for him to speak. As she waited, she took the time to look at him. He had the kind of face most of the girls at school found handsome but dangerous. His hair was cut short and buzzed around the sides of his head. The top of his hair looked as though a hand had run through it repeatedly. The color was another thing that struck Marla: it was such a deep brown color it was almost black. Most people either had brown or black hair, not a coloring that was somehow in the middle.

"Have you found what you're looking for?" The Teacher asked.

"How do you know what I'm looking for?" Marla questioned.

"Because I've looked for them too. It took me a while, but I finally found some. They're not physical, really, but more behavioral, believe it or not. Though there are some physical resemblances."

"Yeah?" Marla asked, sounding just a bit skeptical. "Name two."

"For one, we have the same eyes, nose, and chin. For another, we have the same hair and ears. The big difference is I wear mine as short and wild as possible, and you keep yours long and neat."

"So, we are related?" Marla asked, a slight quiver in her voice. "And that was five, not two, just in case you can't count."

The Teacher gave a light huff and said, "Yeah, you could say we're related. You're my baby sister."

Marla's eyes grew wide as she smiled. "I thought there was some sort of relation, but I didn't think it was this."

"We've been trying to locate you since before your Dad died. Your family's done a great job of hiding you."

"Yeah, they have nothing to do with you not being able to find me. Dad's wife got remarried to some loser. Dad's family wanted nothing to do with her. So, the Bitch and the loser had to start over somewhere else, away from them."

"But what about you?"

"They get to keep me until I'm twenty-one or married. We all know those two aren't going to let me marry anyone they disapprove of, though, I can guarantee that. Those bastards want to be able to control my money."

"We'll see about that. Those two have no idea about our Mom's family: her biological family or Club family."

Marla gulped. "Club?" She asked, not sure if she wanted to know.

"Little One, you are the Princess of the Inferno Wolves MC, whether you know it or not. Grandpa founded the Inferno Wolves. After your Bastard of a father kicked Ma out of their house, she went back to Grandpa. Grandpa took her right back in, no questions asked. She married Axel not long after she returned, and they've been looking for you ever since."

"Wow. I always heard my mother left me behind."

"Just left you behind, are you serious?! Look, we can't talk here. Do you know where Doc's Diner is?"

"I've heard about it," Marla admitted. "That's it."

"Can you meet me there?"

"I have no way of getting there."

"Can you meet me somewhere where I can pick you up, then take you there? We can talk about whatever you want. I'll answer any questions you have."

"Is my Mom here? Can I meet her?" Marla wanted to know.

"Yes, to both of those. And if I don't let Ma know I've finally spoken to you, she's going to kill me herself."

"She wants to see me?" Marla asked, almost afraid to believe what she was hearing.

Marla's newly discovered brother tilted her face up to look at him, putting a hand under Marla's chin.

"Mom hasn't stopped looking for you." He told her.

"Even when people she trusted told her to give up, she refused to stop believing she'd find you. So, when we meet up this afternoon, you're going to be meeting not just me, but Mom, Axel, and our entire family. We have a large damn family, let me tell you."

Marla smiled. "Sounds great; I can't wait to meet everyone." She chuckled, then asked, "What's the Inferno Wolves MC?"

"Love, know you're part of the Wolves, which we can tell you all about when we meet up after school. Now, we're at your next class, so let's get you inside, but before you go, where do you want me to pick you up?"

"How about the gas station on the corner of 10th and Vine? I can get there with no problem."

The Teacher nodded. "I can meet you there, sure. Say at three o'clock?"

"Three's good." Marla agreed, then opened the door to go inside the class.

The History Teacher was standing in front of the class, reciting some of his notes as he wrote what he considered critical points on the chalkboard.

"The class has already started, Miss Petermeire. You're late. You can come back tomorrow." He told her.

"Miss Petermeire was helping me; I'm sorry I'm getting her to you after the bell. She told me she had to get to class, but I told her it wouldn't take long. Unfortunately, it took longer than I thought."

"You're the new Science Teacher, I believe, Mr. Toupin, right?"

"Correct. And I apologize again for getting Miss Petermire here late, that's my fault, but she's the only one that was kind enough to help me carry some of my supplies into the class."

"Well, I guess I can make an exception for her this one time since she was helping another Teacher out. But Miss Petermire, you know the rule: you need to make sure you're here and in your seat before the last bell rings, or you'll be considered absent for the day. Understood?"

"Yes, Sir, Mr. Compo. Thank you for letting me in today." Marla said and quickly took her seat at the back of the class.

"And Mr. Toupin, welcome. If you need more help in the future, I suggest you come before the bell so I can count Miss Petermire in attendance. Her class record is such that I can spare her now and then if she continues to do her work."

Mr. Toupin smiled. "Thank you. I appreciate that. And Miss Petermire, thank you, and you have a good day."

Marla smiled at Mr. Toupin but didn't say anything. She just opened her backpack and started pulling out her binder, and started taking down the notes Mr. Compo had already written down.

The rest of the school day seemed to pass by in a haze. Marla went to each of her classes, doing what she was supposed to, and trying her best to avoid everyone as she didn't want a repeat of what happened with Rebecca earlier in the day.

When the last bell rang for the day, Marla gathered up her supplies and quickly walked to her study class, where she was getting her extra math class, and looked around.

"Spence." Marla greeted one of two people at the school she could consider to be her friend.

"Mar." Spence looked relieved to see her. "Are you okay? Did that Bitch hurt you?"

"Becca? No." Marla said.

"Don't lie to me, Mar." Spence sounded angry.

"I'm not. The Bitch has done worse than that to me many times. But that's not the issue."

"Okay, what is?" Spence wanted to know, raising an eyebrow.

"I need a ride to the house real fast. I have to drop my bag off and pick up my homework for this class. I forgot it on my bed."

"Sure. I'll have Stella take you so no one see's me in the car."

"Thanks."

"No worries. Go, I'll let the Teacher know where you went."

"Okay. I owe you."

"I'll just add it to everything else you owe me."

Marla just shook her head, smiling. She knew Spence had no intention of ever seeking payment for all the things he's helped her with, but one day she had every intention of surprising him with something big. She had no idea what yet, but when she found it, she would just know what it was.

"Don't give me that look," Spence told Marla, trying to look ferocious, and to most people, Marla figured he probably succeeded, though, to her, he looked like a tatted-up teddy bear. Or maybe a watchdog would be more apt to describe him, she thought with his short, dark hair and chiseled face, and his body that all the girls seemed to go crazy over, not that he paid them any attention.

"What look?" Marla asked. "I'm not giving you any look. You're imagining things."

Spence shook his head. "You and Stella are both going to be the death of me, aren't you?" He grumbled.

Marla just looked up at Spence, her eyes wide, and said, "I have no idea what you're talking about."

"Uh-huh, yeah. Sure, you don't." Spence said. "Now hurry up and go meet Stella outside. She'll be by the car."

"Thanks."

"Just get back here safely."

"I will."

With that, Marla quickly hurried out of the class and out to the student parking lot where she saw Stella waiting next to a black, supped-up Dodge Charger playing hard rock over a wholly revamped sound system.

"Sweet!" Marla greeted Stella. "When did Spence put in the new sound system?"

"The day before yesterday. You like it?"

"Are you kidding?!" Marla cried. "I can't believe he didn't tell me."

"He was saving it as a surprise. He knows you and your damn music fixation. He thought you'd like to listen to this when you come over to visit."

Instantly Marla's eyes filled up with tears.

"You're not crying, are you?" Stella demanded.

"Bitch, when have you ever seen me cry?" Marla replied, refusing to let her tears fall.

"Good. I don't want it known my best friend's a softie for music. Or a good deed. I'd have to find a new best friend." Stella joked, but when Marla didn't laugh in return, she looked over at Marla to see if she had inadvertently hurt her feelings.

"Hey, Mar, you okay?" She asked when Marla kept silent.

"Yeah, just surprised Spence did this. He didn't have to."

"Of course, he didn't have to." Stella agreed. "He wanted to. There's a huge difference. And you worry about him and caring for him when everyone else just sees what he can give, which is why he does this. You're his first real friend. Besides me, that is."

That caused Marla to smile. She was lucky to have one friend, let alone a couple of siblings closer than most identical twins.

"Whatever. You know Spence loves me more." Marla told Stella, laughing when she threw a waded-up piece of paper at her, hitting her in the face before she could duck.

"Hey!" Marla cried, feigning injury.

"Suck it up, Buttercup!" Stella shouted, opening the car's door and climbing inside. "Now, get in!"

"Yes, Ma'am!" Marla snapped a quick salute before climbing inside the car herself.

"Good, you're learning. Just remember to keep addressing me like this, and we'll get along famously."

Marla rolled her eyes, her mouth curling up at the edges.

"I saw that smirk," Stella said.

"I don't know what you're talking about," Marla replied.

This time, Stella, who replied, "Whatever," then turned the music up loud as she peeled out of the parking lot and took Marla home to drop off her backpack and pick up her math homework.

At the trailer, as Stella pulled up to a stop, Marla took a deep breath and said, "I'll be right back. You may want to touch up your nails, though. There's no telling if Up Chuck or any of the Bimbos are here to hold me up."

"I thought Chuck and the Bitch from Hell had cars." Stella frowned.

"Not always. It depends on what's going on with those two." A flutter in the window caught Marla's attention. "I'll be out as fast as I can."

"I think I should go up there with you. In case anything goes wrong." Stella said, starting to get out of the car, only to stop when Marla shook her head.

"No, it'll be fine. Just wait here." Marla said again, then hurried over to the door and inside where her uncertain fate awaited her.

CHAPTER 3

The fucking whore looks like a Goddamn three-year-old whose lollipop was taken away with no fucking excuse. Because she didn't get the dick she wanted, she thinks it's everyone else's fault. Like it's our fault, she looks like a fucking dried-up two-cent skank whore too used up to be used for a damn thing. And she thinks adding more damn makeup will make the problems go away? I have words for you Bitch – Revitaline can't erase those lines. But then, who said anything about it being Revitaline?

"You want to tell me who it is waiting for you in that car?" Charles demanded, standing next to Rebecca, waiting for Marla to enter the trailer's front door.

"It's a girl from my math class," Marla replied, unsurprised to see either one of her two tormenters waiting for her.

"Don't fucking lie to me!" Charles shouted.

"I'm not," Marla said. "She just brought me here to get my extra credit work for the after-school math class.

Charles looked at Rebecca, asking, "Well?"

"She's lying. The car belongs to Spencer."

"How would you know if I'm lying or not? Have you been in the car?" Marla asked Rebecca. "Have you seen whose driving?"

Rebecca glared at Marla, her eyes full of hate. "Yes, as a matter of fact, I did see who's driving it. It's pretty hard to miss him when he's blaring that God-awful music."

"You're a damn liar." Marla hissed.

"What did you call me, Runt?" Rebecca demanded just as Chuck grabbed Marla by her throat and lifted her off her feet.

"I dare you to call her that again." He snarled.

"She's lying. She didn't see who's driving the car." Marla choked out. "Or she wants to get me in trouble. Because Stella's out there in the car waiting for me. I'm just trying to get my extra credit work real fast to turn in, and we're going right back to class."

"I don't think so." Chuck smiled. "I need you to clean the kitchen and cook me some food. I'm hungry."

"I have to get back to class," Marla said. "I only have permission to get this work. If I don't get back to the class, they're going to count me absent."

"Then you can miss a fucking day. I told you to clean the fucking kitchen and cook me some Goddamn food, now do it!" Chuck shouted as he tossed Marla down onto the floor, causing her to hit her head against the wall when she landed.

A knock sounded on the door just as it pushed open, and Stella popped her head inside.

"Hey, Girlie, what's the holdup?" Stella asked, trying to act as if she was oblivious to what was going on in front of her. "We have to hurry. We only have ten more minutes to get back to class, chop, chop. Oh, hi, Mr. Petermeire. It's good to see you again. I'm sorry, but Mar and I really must hurry and get back to class. We're just grabbing some extra credit we've been working on so we can turn it in then go on to some new work." Stella looked over at Marla and raised a brow. "Are you coming, or are you going to keep the floor company?"

"Yeah, I just tripped. I'll be right there." Marla told her, slowly standing up and trying to make her way back to the living room where her homework was sitting next to the couch.

"No, you're not," Rebecca said. "You were told to clean the kitchen then cook us some food."

"No, Chuck told me to cook him some food. Not you. So, here's an idea. Why don't you cook him some food since you're so anxious to eat? Because if I don't go to this Class, Chuck and your Mom are the ones going to be held responsible." Marla smiled. "And you know they'll love getting fined for me not going to class."

Chuck didn't look happy hearing reminders about fines for Marla missing a mandatory tutoring class. "Why the hell didn't you say so?"

He demanded. "Hurry up and get out of here. Becca will clean up and fix me some food instead."

Rebecca gasped. "Like fuck I will. I'm not your fucking slave. You want food, get it your damn self."

Reaching out a hand, Chuck grabbed hold of Rebecca's hair and forced her to her knees.

"You will do what I tell you to if you know what the fuck is good for you. You understand me?"

As Rebecca and Chuck fought to see who was the more Alpha between the two of them, Marla and Stella quietly backed out of the trailer to avoid getting caught in the middle of their battle. They had places to go, people to see, and school was just the beginning.

Once in the car, and Stella was sure they were a safe distance away from the war zone, she turned to Marla and demanded, "Okay, now tell me what the hell that was all about."

"The hell if I know. There's always drama at my place if you haven't realized that by now. No matter what we do or where we go, we end up in trouble."

"That's true. Now, are you going to tell me why you just had to go home and get your extra credit when it's not due for an extra three weeks?"

"I told Spence I had to get it, but that was an excuse. I had to get out of school. I'm meeting someone at the gas station at the corner of 10th and Vine. Can you drop me off there? I can give you a few bucks for gas."

"And you didn't tell Spence? Why?" Stella wanted to know.

"Because I couldn't let the teacher know where I was going, and if Spence didn't know I was skipping, he couldn't get in trouble."

Stella shook her head. "I appreciate you were trying to protect my brother, but Spence is not going to be happy. He's going to be pissed when he finds out what you did."

"He'll forgive me."

"Of course. But it's going to cost you a LOT of Red Bulls and Mt. Dews. You know that, right?" Stella said, laughing, turning to go to the gas station instead of the school.

Five minutes later, Marla and Stella pulled up to the gas station and walked inside to get a drink and snack while Marla looked around to make sure she didn't miss seeing anyone she was supposed to meet.

Once she was sure no one was there, she went inside and looked around as Stella grabbed what she wanted. At the cash register, Stella paid for all but a couple of items. When she finished paying, Stella walked away from the counter as the cashier rang the last couple of things up and told Marla, "$3.29."

"Excuse me?" Marla replied, confused.

The cashier looked at Marla and said, "It's $3.29. Are you going to pay it by cash or card?"

Stella spoke up. "It'll be cash. Hey, Mar, I'm not going to take your gas money. Get the snack, and let's wait for your mystery, man. It's getting hotter than well digger's ass here. We need to go somewhere cool, so let's get going already."

Marla just nodded. She knew why Stella was doing this, and she appreciated her help, but she was still going to give her the change, regardless of what she said; charity was not something Marla was ever going to accept; it didn't matter what the intentions.

CHAPTER 4

The fucking whore looks like a Goddamn three-year-old whose lollipop was taken away with no fucking excuse. Because she didn't get the dick she wanted, she thinks it's everyone else's fault. Like it's our fault, she looks like a fucking dried-up two-cent skank whore too used up to be used for a damn thing. And she thinks adding more damn makeup will make the problems go away? I have words for you Bitch – Revitaline can't erase those lines. But then, who said anything about it being Revitaline?

"You want to tell me who it is waiting for you in that car?" Charles demanded, standing next to Rebecca, waiting for Marla to enter the trailer's front door.

"It's a girl from my math class," Marla replied, unsurprised to see either one of her two tormenters waiting for her.

"Don't fucking lie to me!" Charles shouted.

"I'm not," Marla said. "She just brought me here to get my extra credit work for the after-school math class.

Charles looked at Rebecca, asking, "Well?"

"She's lying. The car belongs to Spencer."

"How would you know if I'm lying or not? Have you been in the car?" Marla asked Rebecca. "Have you seen whose driving?"

Rebecca glared at Marla, her eyes full of hate. "Yes, as a matter of fact, I did see who's driving it. It's pretty hard to miss him when he's blaring that God-awful music."

"You're a damn liar." Marla hissed.

"What did you call me, Runt?" Rebecca demanded just as Chuck grabbed Marla by her throat and lifted her off her feet.

"I dare you to call her that again." He snarled.

"She's lying. She didn't see who's driving the car." Marla choked out. "Or she wants to get me in trouble. Because Stella's out there in the car waiting for me. I'm just trying to get my extra credit work real fast to turn in, and we're going right back to class."

"I don't think so." Chuck smiled. "I need you to clean the kitchen and cook me some food. I'm hungry."

"I have to get back to class," Marla said. "I only have permission to get this work. If I don't get back to the class, they're going to count me absent."

"Then you can miss a fucking day. I told you to clean the fucking kitchen and cook me some Goddamn food, now do it!" Chuck shouted as he tossed Marla down onto the floor, causing her to hit her head against the wall when she landed.

A knock sounded on the door just as it pushed open, and Stella popped her head inside.

"Hey, Girlie, what's the holdup?" Stella asked, trying to act as if she was oblivious to what was going on in front of her. "We have to hurry. We only have ten more minutes to get back to class, chop, chop. Oh, hi, Mr. Petermeire. It's good to see you again. I'm sorry, but Mar and I really must hurry and get back to class. We're just grabbing some extra credit we've been working on so we can turn it in then go on to some new work." Stella looked over at Marla and raised a brow. "Are you coming, or are you going to keep the flooring company?"

"Yeah, I just tripped. I'll be right there." Marla told her, slowly standing up and trying to make her way back to the living room where her homework was sitting next to the couch.

"No, you're not," Rebecca said. "You were told to clean the kitchen then cook us some food."

"No, Chuck told me to cook him some food. Not you. So, here's an idea. Why don't you cook him some food since you're so anxious to eat? Because if I don't go to this Class, Chuck and your Mom are the ones going to be held responsible." Marla smiled. "And you know they'll love getting fined for me not going to class."

Chuck didn't look happy hearing reminders about fines for Marla missing a mandatory tutoring class. "Why the hell didn't you say so?"

He demanded. "Hurry up and get out of here. Becca will clean up and fix me some food instead."

Rebecca gasped. "Like fuck I will. I'm not your fucking slave. You want food, get it your damn self."

Reaching out a hand, Chuck grabbed hold of Rebecca's hair and forced her to her knees.

"You will do what I tell you to if you know what the fuck is good for you. You understand me?"

As Rebecca and Chuck fought to see who was the more Alpha between the two of them, Marla and Stella quietly backed out of the trailer to avoid getting caught in the middle of their battle. They had places to go, people to see, and school was just the beginning.

Once in the car, and Stella was sure they were a safe distance away from the war zone, she turned to Marla and demanded, "Okay, now tell me what the hell that was all about."

"The hell if I know. There's always drama at my place if you haven't realized that by now. No matter what we do or where we go, we end up in trouble."

"That's true. Now, are you going to tell me why you just had to go home and get your extra credit when it's not due for an extra three weeks?"

"I told Spence I had to get it, but that was an excuse. I had to get out of school. I'm meeting someone at the gas station at the corner of 10th and Vine. Can you drop me off there? I can give you a few bucks for gas."

"And you didn't tell Spence? Why?" Stella wanted to know.

"Because I couldn't let the teacher know where I was going, and if Spence didn't know I was skipping, he couldn't get in trouble."

Stella shook her head. "I appreciate you were trying to protect my brother, but Spence is not going to be happy. He's going to be pissed when he finds out what you did."

"He'll forgive me."

"Of course. But it's going to cost you a LOT of Red Bulls and Mt. Dews. You know that, right?" Stella said, laughing, turning to go to the gas station instead of the school.

Five minutes later, Marla and Stella pulled up to the gas station and walked inside to get a drink and snack while Marla looked around to make sure she didn't miss seeing anyone she was supposed to meet.

Once she was sure no one was there, she went inside and looked around as Stella grabbed what she wanted. At the cash register, Stella paid for all but a couple of items. When she finished paying, Stella walked away from the counter as the cashier rang the last couple of things up and told Marla, "$3.29."

"Excuse me?" Marla replied, confused.

The cashier looked at Marla and said, "It's $3.29. Are you going to pay it by cash or card?"

Stella spoke up. "It'll be cash. Hey, Mar, I'm not going to take your gas money. Get the snack, and let's wait for your mystery, man. It's getting hotter than well digger's ass here. We need to go somewhere cool, so let's get going already."

Marla just nodded. She knew why Stella was doing this, and she appreciated her help, but she was still going to give her the change, regardless of what she said; charity was not something Marla was ever going to accept; it didn't matter what the intentions.

CHAPTER 5

It's hilarious how much these bitches think they can get just by shaking their cellulite-infused asses at any intelligence impaired Neanderthal.
Though that's probably insulting the Neanderthal's on my part. These guys allow the tramps to make cuckolds of them half the fucking time and seem to enjoy it. Still, I have to say this makes for some good laughs when I feel like shoving
burning charcoal down my fucking throat.
The good part is this shit isn't going to last too much longer. There's a surprise coming
the likes of these bastards ain't never seen, and I can't wait to see their faces. Oh, the joy there will be when these pricks start to
come crawling over to me when they realize I hold the cards to everything they want. Oh, wait, they won't be able to! These fuckers will be in pieces, spread out like a fucking jigsaw puzzle!

The ride out of town took an hour and a half, and Marla spent her time holding on to Bret as tightly as she could, watching everything as if it was the first time, and for a lot of what she saw, it was; especially when they came upon the fortress, the Club called their Compound.

"Hey, Little One, what has you so uptight right now, if you don't mind me asking?" Bret asked through the headset inside the helmet he put on Marla's head just before they mounted his bike and everyone took off, heading out of town.

"You're crazy if you think this is uptight," Marla replied.

"Well, in this case, your body's lying on you," Bret told her gently, though Marla could hear the smile in his voice. "You can hold onto me a bit lighter if you want by just grabbing the shirt or just lightly wrapping your arms around me. You don't need to squeeze. And when we make a turn, press the top of your body against mine. Lean against me until you're ready to sit back on your own. Or you can just lean into a turn while holding onto my shirt. Just do me a favor and try not to strangle me!" Bret laughed.

Marla eased up on her hold a bit, trying not to make it obvious she was staring at all the buildings behind the gate, especially the house that looked almost like a castle.

"You live here?" Marla asked as everyone slowly came to a stop in a large oval driveway.

"Well, Mom, Axel, and Gramps do. The rest of the guys and I live in the houses behind this one. We're all spread out on the property. The buildings you see at the front are part of the club businesses. It's where we build custom cars and motorcycles. Our repair shops are in the cities, but if you want an actual car built by our company, this is where we make the magic happen."

"Well, shit," Marla said, both awed and saddened at the same time.

"What?" Bret asked once they started toward the main group.

"Spence will never leave here. And the worst part is, I won't be able to get far enough away!" Marla laughed. "Me and Spence's wet dreams don't go in the same damn sentence! That's just ew!"

"Ok, TMI, as you kids say! I don't need to know about your friends' sex life."

"That's too bad," Spence joked. "You're going to be hearing a hell of a lot about it since I have no intention of leaving here. And I do mean here," Spence motioned to where he was standing. "Because I'll be too fucking busy jerking off at the cars you all are building."

"Alright, Spence, what was it I told you about you, me, your dreams, yadda, yadda, and so forth? Is it this time or next time I am supposed to kick your ass?"

Spence gulped, walked over to Marla, and wrapped an arm around her waist. "Have I told you you're my favorite sister? Just don't tell Stella. She thinks she's still my favorite, and I don't want to hurt her feelings."

"Of course, you don't want me to find out, you ass! How long have you been cheating on me, you prick?!" Stella demanded, marching up to Marla and Spence. "What, I'm not good enough or something?"

Spence laughed. "Truly?" He asked as Stella got right up in his face. "For favorite? Right now? No, you're not. Did you see the beauty they just drug out of that building back there?! But you ask who's my favorite when it's time to put that beauty together, it's you, hands down. I wouldn't dare let the Brat within thousand miles of her."

"Hey now!" Marla objected. "I am not that bad. And I deserve to be the favorite sister now, or I may just have to stop working and tell the owner I refuse the promotion to manager."

Both Spence and Stella looked at Marla, and their mouths dropped open.

"Are you serious?" Stella demanded, jumping on Marla and holding her close. "Old Man Johnson is finally stepping down and letting you take over after school and on weekends?"

Marla grinned. "I was going to tell you assholes later this afternoon, but since you can't figure out if I'm the favorite sister or not, I guess it doesn't matter."

"Doesn't matter, my ass!" Stella shrieked, looking over at Spence, who nodded. "We're going to take care of your family issues right now: get to know your Mom and brother, talk to the police, figure out our sleeping arrangements, and everything else. Sound g…" She was interrupted as if on cue by Marla's phone, screaming Eminem's "97 Bonnie and Clyde".

"Talk about a fucking buzz kill," Stella muttered. "You going to answer that?" She asked when Marla just looked up at her and Spence.

"Do I have a choice?" Marla quipped. "He's only going to start constantly calling if I don't pick up."

"Put it on speaker. I want to hear everything this douchebag has to say to you. Got it?"

"Got it, Mother." Marla rolled her eyes, smiling, then frowned as she pulled her phone from her backpack and answered it as it began ringing for a second time.

"Charlie…" Marla began only to be cut off by Chuck, who started his screaming tirade immediately.

"Where the fuck are you, you little bitch?!" He demanded. "What the fuck did you think you were doin'? Did you think you could spread your fuckin' legs for those bastards, and I wouldn't know? You're just like your whore of a mother. Only she wasn't much of a whore after your dad got done teachin' her a few lessons. Now it looks like you'll be learnin' a few of her fuckin' lessons yourself when Sal gets here. So, if you don't want any of your new friends to get up close and personal with Jesus, I fuckin' suggest you get that pretty pussy back here where it belongs. NOW!"

Marla collapsed, trying to speak but unable to say a word. Her eyes that had been joking with her friends and alive with her newly acquainted brother just minutes before instantly went dead. To hear her nightmare spoken aloud was not something she was ready for, even though she was sure Spence and Stella both were already aware of what was going on: ignorance is bliss. If she didn't acknowledge anything happening, then that meant nothing was happening.

Stella hurriedly picked up the phone as Marla dropped it next to her, while Spence wrapped his arms around Marla and tried to hold her close, only the instant she felt masculine hands on her she tensed up and started fighting to get away, screaming at the top of her lungs.

"Get away from me! Don't touch me! Don't touch me! Don't!"

Melodie rushed up to Marla and knelt in front of her. She held her hands held out so that Marla could lean against her if she chose.

"Marla, Baby Girl, it's your Mother. Marla, listen to my voice. Marla, Charlie lied to you. Your Dad never "taught me any lessons," I promise you. Your Dad was a business control conglomerate, but he never lifted a hand to me. He wasn't that kind of person. And he absolutely loved you. You were everything to him. Can you hear me, Baby?" Melodie asked soothingly.

Still kneeling in front of Marla, Melodie kept her hands where Marla could always see them, though she asked, "Baby, can I touch your hair real quick?"

Marla didn't respond; whimpers were all the answers she gave while at the same time, Stella was shouting at Charlie.

"You Goddamn fucking, child molester. Your sorry ass better hope I never see you again, or I swear to fucking God, I will kill you myself! Do you understand me, you fucking piece of shit?! There's not a large enough rock to hide your pathetic ass, you Bastard! So, you better start looking for ways to get out of this fucking country if you want hope of salvaging your minuscule cum launcher because it's what I'm going to be feeding to the fucking piranhas' at the Goddamn kiddies living history museum!" Screaming by the time she ended the threats, Stella watched as the men cupped their groins, groaning.

Bret hurried over and took the phone out of Stella's hands, squeezing so hard he almost broke it in half with his hand.

"You listen to me, you sick son of a bitch," Bret snarled. "Marla is staying right where she is. You will never get a chance to see her or talk to her ever again, and you sure as hell will never get the opportunity to touch her. Do I make myself clear? There will be some very unpleasant consequences if you attempt otherwise."

There was a second pause before Charlie demanded, "Who the fuck do you think you are?"

"I'm Bret Toupin, and I believe you know who I am, but in case you don't, let me make it clear. I am Marla's older brother, and she will be residing with her biological family from now on. Try to stop her, and you will be starting a war with the largest MC Club this side of the Mississippi. That's not to mention all the Club's alliances."

"You don't know what you've done. Sal and Timon ain't gonna let her go, and they sure as hell ain't gonna let some wannabe boys club take what's their's."

"This Sal and Timon are welcome to come and try to get her. Just know, they won't be the only ones to die when the shit hits the fan."

"You can't fucking threaten me!" Charlie shouted over the phone.

"It's not a fucking threat," Bret replied. "It's a promise." He continued, then hung up.

Once he disconnected with Charlie, Bret looked over at his father and the Detective standing next to him.

"This Charlie fellow is sending Salvatore and Timon our way," Bret told them. "We need to prepare for shit to get ugly."

Axel glanced at Rip and Snake, who were both walking up to their group, then spoke.

"Let's get everyone inside. Bret, make sure everyone who has family gets them here, see that they're safely inside our walls. I want everyone to stay within the Compound walls. I need all Officers to meet in ten. Spence, Stella, you're going to join us."

"I need to take Marla to her room so she can lay down, but when I come out, I'm going to join you and screw your Church rules. Especially if Spence and Stella are joining you." Melodie told her husband. She looked at Spence and Stella. "Will you tell us what you know of Marla's past, and this Sal and Timon when I get back?" She asked, gently taking Marla's hand in her own, making sure Marla wouldn't start screaming the entire time.

Stella nodded. "Yes," She said. "I'm not sure exactly how much we know, but we can tell you what it is we do—Marla's extremely private, even with us to a degree."

"That's understandable. With everything Marla's been through, she would learn to become a private person. But the three of you are close, and that would have earned you some of her trust. I'm not asking you to betray any of her confidence; you can't do that. I am asking that you extend some of that trust to us and help us start making some decisions. The guys can't do anything against Salvatore or Timon if we don't know what to expect."

"We'll do what we can." Spence agreed for Stella and him.

"Thank you," Melodie said. "Now go follow the guys to their man-cave. I'll follow you there shortly."

With that, Melodie gently escorted Marla away from the group of bikers and into the large house. The house loomed in front of everyone. The large pillars and wrap-around veranda made it look like a giant southern plantation. Stella wondered if it was as old as it looked or if they made it to look that way.

Walking inside with Marla, Melodie heard all of the men grumbling about her man-cave comment making her smile. She knew Axel would bitch about it the most this evening when the two of them are alone, something she looked forward to, shivering with delight.

CHAPTER 6

If these bastards think for one second, I am going to roll over, they had better think again. Especially when I decide it's time to take my game to the next fucking level. Who the fuck am I? The sons-of-bitches created me, yet they think they can so easily just throw me to the side and forget about what they've done? I don't fucking think so! And after what I'm about to do to them, they will never forget about me.

Once inside the house, Melodie began leading Marla towards the staircase that stood slightly to the doorway's right but paused when she noticed her father waiting.

"Pops," she greeted. "I take it you heard the screams."

"It sounded like you're murdering someone out there."

"You wouldn't be that far from the truth, unfortunately," Melodie told him. "It turns out due to some prior trauma and a fucked up conversation, Marla was just triggered."

"Marla? Dear God, she looks just like you when you were her age."

"I know, Pops." Melodie gave a small smile. "It's eerie how close we look like each other."

"Surprising, because you looked nothing like your Mom."

Melodie shrugged. "What can I say? I drew the short end of the stick and got to look like you."

"I thought our girl's name is Marcie."

"Marla is the name she grew up knowing, and that is the name she asked us to call her. But, I think, considering everything she's been through right now, proper introductions should wait until she's feeling better. What do you say, Pops?"

"Go, take your girl to her room, and get her settled. I can meet her properly when she's rested. Just make sure you take care of her right."

Melodie rolled her eyes at her father. "Yes, Dad. Anything else you want me to do while I'm taking care of her, for you ?"

"Yeah, mind your sass, girl. You're not too big I can't turn you over my knee and wallop you some."

Marla shrank back against Melodie, whimpering.

"Easy," Melodie said, tightening an arm wrapped around Marla's waist. "Easy there. You're safe. Pop's is just joking. He's not going to hurt anyone, I promise you."

Melodie turned to look at her Dad with sorrow-filled eyes. "I need to get Marla up to her room. I'll be back down shortly."

"Go." He gestured up the stairs. "I'll be waiting down here with the guys when you come back down."

"We're all going to meet in your Boy's Club when I get back down. Two of Marla's friends are outside with the guys, and they'll be at the meeting. They're going to tell us some of what is going on, so we're not blind-sided."

"Then I'm going to get a damn drink. It's five o'clock somewhere in this fucking world."

"Language, Pops," Melodie grumbled, turning to guide Marla silently up the stairs.

At the top of the stairs, Melodie turned to the left. Walking to the end of the hall, she paused at the last door on the right then opened the door to enter the room.

"Here you go, Love," Melodie told Marla. "Let's get you in bed, and then I'm going to go speak to Axel and everyone. I'm not letting them make any decisions without me there. Up you go."

Helping Marla onto the bed, Melodie removed Marla's shoes and pulled the covers from underneath her to cover her up.

"Here you go. I'll be back in a bit to check on you. You just rest and feel better. I love you, Baby Girl." Melody told her.

As she left the room, Melody left the door cracked. There was no way she would leave Marla alone in a room with the door completely shut, in the condition her daughter was currently in. Once Melodie got to Church, she would have one of the Prospects sit outside of her room. That way, when Marla got up, if the girl needed any help, someone would be readily accessible.

Melodie made her way back downstairs to where everyone was waiting to hear what Stella and Spence had to say.

"Good, you didn't start without me," Melodie said, only half-joking.

"And get a knife lodged in my balls later? Are you kidding?" Axel demanded. "You just got your girl back. There's no fucking way I'm going to stand between you and anything that goes on with her."

Melodie walked up to Axel and patted his cheek. "Smart man." She smiled.

"Now," she turned to face the twins. "Which one of you wants to start telling us what's going on? Wait," she quickly changed the subject.

"Before we begin, Pops, have you met Marla's friends Stella and Spence? Stella, Spence, this is my father, Daelan Hughes. He's the founder of Inferno Wolves

MC and the founder and CEO of DaHughes Choppers and Roadsters, but everyone calls him Digger. I think he's someone you would like to get to know, Spence, so after we're done talking here, how about you get to know him?"

Spence looked like he just won the million-dollar lottery for a second before someone stole the ticket from him. "Really?" He asked, embarrassed. "It's not like I'm a kid. I don't need any handouts."

"Of course you don't, boyo," Daelan said. "The question isn't whether you're a kid or not. The question is whether or not we're going to do what men do and bond over drinks and machinery." Daelan spoke up.

Glancing at Daelan, Spence gave a curt nod. If there were even one iota of a chance he would be able to spend some time with his idol and learn more about cars, he was going to take the opportunity.

"Great," Melodie said, satisfied. "Now, will one of you two kids , please tell us what is going on with this Salvatore and Timon?" She continued, stressing the word 'kids' to get her point across and earning a glare from each of them.

Stella didn't even glance at Spence when she stood up and said, "Fine. We'll tell you whatever you want to know, as long as it has nothing to do with Marla. If you're going to get any information about her, you have to ask her, not be some chicken shit pussies and get it by going to everyone around her."

Axel growled. "I'd watch who you call pussies, little girl. You'll find you'll come across someone bigger and meaner than you one day, and you sure as hell won't like it."

"When Marla's better, and you refuse to ask her any of your questions because you're afraid of hurting her, then that's what you are. And you sure as fuck won't be helping her. Just don't ask her any stupid questions like, 'were you molested' because that sure as fuck will send her over the edge."

Stepping right in front of Stella's face, Axel growled menacingly. "Who the hell do you think you are?"

"I'm Marla's best friend!" Stella shouted right back at him. "I've known and loved her since she was nine years old! I will not just stand idly by with a stick up my fucking ass and let anyone hurt her, including you!"

Grunting, Axel took a step back and looked Stella up and down as Spence walked up to Stella and wrapped her in his arms, trying to soothe her.

"You don't want to go against Mr. Toupin like you have either of Salvatore or Timon's men."

Stella snorted. "They weren't men, they were…"

"I know, but the only reason they haven't come after you yet is that they haven't realized Marla's best friend and the girl that killed three of their men is the same girl. Once they do, they will come after you with everything."

"I'd like to see them try. I'm this close," Stella held her thumb and index finger together. "To finding Uncle Jack and Uncle Tate. They're not dead, and the military keeps telling us they'll look for them. For nine years? Fuck that. They're hiding some fucking shit while we're stuck in this Goddamn hell hole, and Marla's paying the fucking price. You know Jack and Tate wouldn't leave us if they knew what happened."

"I know. What happened this time?" Spence asked.

"The bastard sold my computer this time; he didn't just hock the damn thing."

"We'll get you another one. You can keep it in the trunk or something – we'll figure it out."

Trying to follow their conversation, Axel finally had enough. Letting out a loud whistle, he let out an audible sigh and said, "Good, now that I have your attention, did we just understand you to have killed three men girl? And why? And why would you be looking for your uncles for nine years in the military? If they're in the military, you just get a Red Cross SOS message to them, and they'll either call you or come get you, not leave you for nine years. So they're probably not in the military any longer."

"The fuck buckets I killed were just that. They held me down at one point and tried to rape me after they roughed me up a bit. I managed to grab one of their guns and use it on them. They didn't think I had the guts to do that, said I was too much of a girl. Well, I showed them. I pointed it right at each of them without flinching and pulled the fucking trigger. I have the gun in my backpack. As for our Uncles, they're still alive, and they're still in the Navy. They're SEALs. That's part of the problem. The other part of the problem is either the Navy is hiding them or the Government in general. Every time I get close to contacting either of them, I get kicked out of the room I'm in. They also shut down the server just to make sure I can't get back in. I have to keep retrying."

"That does sound like they're hiding. And you're sure your Uncles have no idea about what's going on with either of you?" Daelan asked from where he was sitting.

"No, they would never leave us like this. There was a fight between our Uncles and our Grandparents, but we were all extremely close before that. And our Grandparents regretted the fight ever since it happened."

"What about your parents? What did they think?" Axel wanted to know.

"Our parents died in a car accident shortly after we were born. Our Grandparents and Uncles raised us until our Uncles joined the Navy, then it was just our Grandparents."

"Alright. Stella, I want you to go with one of our newer guys and show him what you've done so far. Let's see if he can't help you try to reach your Uncles. Spence, you stay here and answer some questions for us. Let's see how productive we can make the rest of this day." Axel shook his head. "I need a damn drink."

"Let's get through this, and then we can let the drinks fly," Melodie said, laying her head on Axel's chest.

"Not tonight. The bar is open if anyone is interested. When Marla is up and feeling better, then we can have a party and drinks for those that are interested."

"That sounds like a good idea. I think a barbeque is something we could all use." Melodie agreed, kissing Axel softly on the lips.

"I agree. Now, let's get this over with so you can start planning everything."

Melodie looked at Stella and rolled her eyes, smiling. "It's cute how these men think they're the ones in charge of things. Whatever happens in life, don't ever give up your independence or your self-respect. They're the two most important things you have as a woman, regardless of what anyone else ever tries to tell you. Family and a sense of belonging come next."

Stella waited for Axel to show her who was going to help her. She never had help before locating her Uncles, and now she had a good feeling about this.

"Who am I supposed to go with?" Stella asked, completely ignoring what Melodie had to say.

Axel tilted his head to the door that opened behind the group. "That would be my man Gunner. He just came in. He's also my best IT guy. If it requires anything to do with computers, he's the man for the job."

"Is he the person that found Marla?" Stella wanted to know.

"Yes. However, Gunner was training someone to help him."

"Where is he?"

"Back in L.A. His mother is sick, and he went home to help take care of her."

"Oh," Stella said.

"You say that like you're surprised." Axel smiled.

"I am," Stella admitted, smiling back sheepishly, which caused Axel to laugh.

"Don't worry. Even big bad bikers have soft spots for our mothers. Just don't let it be known we go out of our way to help them."

"I won't. So, I go with your gun-totin' nerd. Got it. If he's as good as you say he is, we should find my Uncles in no time, thank you."

"Go take care of what you need to and get back. Hopefully, you'll have some good news to share when you do."

Stella nodded, then turned to walk to the back of the room where the newcomer stood at the door, grinning.

"Gun-totin' nerd, huh?" Gunner asked teasing, which caused Stella to blush.

Stella shrugged. "You're covered in guns, both literally and figuratively, and you're a genius at computers? You're a gun-totin' nerd. People don't see too many of those around except maybe in the military. Even then, they're usually in the Special Forces."

"You're pretty smart for a kid. You know that?" Gunner asked, a bit more than impressed.

"Maybe." Stella agreed. "But all Marla and I do are read, study, and work. And fight with her so-called family. Going to the library and watching videos about the Special Forces or reading all the books about Special Forces we could find is a real treat."

"Well, if you have any questions about the SEALS, just ask: I will tell you what I can. Doc, who's back in Church, while being a SEAL, worked with the Force Recon. If you ask him, he'll be happy to answer some of your questions too. Now, here we are. Let me input my passcode, and voila! All the nerdy tech your heart desires! What do you think? Is there enough here to help you try to locate your Uncles?"

Stella looked around the room, her mouth hanging open. This room had everything she could ever hope to have one day, and more! The computers and screens were beyond anything she had ever imagined.

"You're going to let me help you work on these computers?" Stella asked Gunner, her voice full of disbelief.

"Sure, you're going to show me where you went and how far you got before you got kicked out. Then I'll either take over for you or walk you through what we need to do next."

Stella looked surprised. "You'd let me help instead of doing it for me?"

"Of course. Why wouldn't I?"

"I don't know. Most people wouldn't. They'd just do the job themselves and tell me to watch."

"Well, I'm not most people, so sit your ass down in that chair there and get comfortable. I have a feeling we're going to be here for a while."

"Yeah, probably," Stella admitted. "The last time I did this, I was at this over five hours."

"Unless their firewalls are that good, it shouldn't take us that long."

"If you say so." Stella sounded skeptical.

Gunner smirked. "Go," he said smirking. "Sit down and get to work. You'll see what I'm talking about."

Sitting down as quickly as possible, Stella hurried in front of the computers. Her fingers flew over the keyboards. Instantly Stella began repeating the work she had done so often in the past, getting lost in what she considered her new love.

Three hours later, Stella sat back and said, "Okay, your turn. I keep getting stuck here."

"You did great." Gunner said, impressed. "You got a lot farther than I thought you would. Now let me see how much farther I can take this, and we'll call this done."

Another four hours went by when Gunner finally let out a loud whoop, which woke up Stella, sleeping on his couch.

"Did you get anything?" Stella asked groggily.

"Sure did. I just got a reply from someone called Devastation. This person says they know both Jack and Tate, and they will pass a message along to them. They said if Jack and Tate know you, and you're who you're claiming to be, then they will contact us in a few minutes."

No sooner than he spoke, a shrill ringing sounded, indicating an incoming call.

Quickly reaching over, Gunner answered the call.

"Talk to me." Gunner said.

"I was told you have a Stella and Spence Hunter there. Is that true?"

"It is. I have Stella right next to me. Give me a second, and I will hand the phone to her. May I tell her who's calling?" Gunner asked.

"Tell her Jack and Tate are on the phone for her."

"Very well. Stella, I'm putting the phone on speaker, is that okay?"

"Yes."

"It's all yours. I'm here for any questions you will have."

"Thanks."

Before anyone could say anything else, Stella cried, "Uncle Tate! I've tried to get ahold of you for so long!"

"Stella? Baby? Is it really you?" Tate sounded as if he couldn't believe what he was hearing.

"I've tried so hard to look for you two. If Gunner didn't help me, I was going to give up. I had no other means of searching."

"Our number is unlisted, I know. I'm sorry. Is Spence there? What about Gram and Gramps? Where are they?"

"Spence is with our hosts. I'll get him. He wants to speak to you too. He asks me all the time if I managed to contact you yet. Gram and Gramps, though? They aren't here."

Jack joined the conversation. "It's great to hear your voice, love. But what do you mean, Gram and Gramps aren't there? Where are they?"

"Uncle Jack!" Stella greeted him joyously.

"Love?" Jack asked again.

"They died," Stella said softly. "They died nine years ago in a fucking car accident."

"WHAT?!" The two uncles shouted.

"Just after your fight. They went out for their date night, and on their way back, a drunk driver hit them. Grams died right away, but Gramps died as they tried to take him to the hospital."

"Why didn't anyone reach out to us through the Red Cross?" Tate demanded.

"We tried. The Navy told the State they would try to get a hold of you. I have copies of all correspondence. We never heard anything."

"No one ever reached out to us. This is the first we've ever heard anything about Grams and Gramps dying. If they're gone, where have you been staying?"

"Spence and I are in a foster house. We've been with them since the accident."

"Dear God," Jack muttered when Tate swore.

"And Gunner, how are you involved?" Tate wanted to know.

"I'm a member of…" Gunner began, only to be cut off.

"He's a family member of our best friend. After being separated for years, she was just reunited with her biological family. We're all here getting to know each other."

A loud banging on the door interrupted the conversation.

"Gunner, open up!" Axel shouted from outside the computer room.

"Opening!" Gunner replied. "What's going on?" He asked.

"We have a situation. The Bitch who kept Marla is here. She brought the Police with her. Sitting in a car across the street is none other than Salvatore and Timon."

Jack spoke up, joining the conversation. "Salvatore and Timon? You don't mean Salvatore Guarnieri and Timon Valdovinos do you?"

Axel shrugged, then realized Jack couldn't see his response over the phone and said, "I don't know. Stella, are those the Bastards last names?"

"Yes. And if those Bastards are waiting across the street, Marla won't make it to the Bitch's house or the Police Station. Sal's here to take her now."

"The fuck he will." Axel snarled. "No one is taking my woman's daughter from her again. Not after she just got the girl back!"

Stella looked up at Axel, tears in her eyes. "Are you prepared to die, to keep her here? Because that's what it will take."

"Damn right, I am. And so are my men. We're a family, and we make damn sure we watch each other's back!"

"Jack and I will be there in five hours. Can you hold these people off until we get there?" Tate asked.

"And just who the fuck are you?" Axel asked.

"We're Stella and Spence's Uncles. Let's just say we're part of a sub-group of the Special Forces."

Axel's head jerked up. "The Covert Teams."

"All Special Forces are covert, yes. We have to be."

"We'll hold them off. Five hours is nothing."

"Keep us on the phone while you go deal with this woman and the Police. We'd like to hear what they have to say." Tate told Axel.

"Sure. Gunner, you and Stella come with me. Let's get this shit over with."

"Stella," Tate said, switching the conversation back to his niece. "As soon as we're done, we're flying out after we say hi to Spence. I will text Gunner our phone numbers, so you have them; call us at any time."

"Thank you, Uncle Tate," Stella said.

"You don't need to thank us. You should have been with us."

"You're coming to get us now. That's all that matters." Stella paused. "We're about to enter the lobby."

"Okay. Keep quiet, no matter what happens or what you hear. Do you understand?"

"I can't promise that."

"Stella. Do you understand?" Tate repeated. "These people are dangerous.

"No, shit. We've lived with these Bastards for the past nine years."

As the group walked into the front lobby, Annie stood in the hallway, screaming. Her hair was disheveled, and there were black smudges all over her face.

"She killed my family! I want her arrested for blowing up my fucking home!" Annie screamed, trying desperately to reach Melodie but was held back by two Police Officers.

"Mrs. Petermiere, if you don't settle down, we're going to have to ask you to leave." One of the Police Officers told the struggling woman.

"She wanted my daughter and couldn't have her, so she killed her! What are you going to do about it?!" Annie demanded, struggling even more desperately to try and break free of the Police Officers' hold.

"I would have loved to kill those pieces of shit you call family." Melodie sneered. "Unfortunately, I've been here taking care of business. You can look at security tapes if you need to verify that. However, I'll be going out to drink over the fact they're dead once you're gone, you fucking whore. Given the fact you kidnapped my daughter and held her fucking hostage for thirteen Goddamn years! And that you let your fucking husband MOLEST her! And let's not forget about the fact your husband sold her to the Italian Mob! Do you want me to go on?!"

"How dare you?!" Annie screamed. "Now she's lying on top of killing my family! Why the fuck aren't you lazy sons-of-bitches doing anything?!"

One of the Police Officers stepped forward and pushed Annie's arms back as he apologized to Melodie.

"I'm sorry, Mrs. Toupin, but we have to do our job. Where were you three hours ago?"

"I've been here, taking care of my daughter and the logs for the DaHughes Choppers and Roadsters."

"You said there's video surveillance of you here?" The Police Officer asked.

"Absolutely. It's always on when we're working with company business, either in the house or outside. It's how our insurance covers us."

"Would you mind letting us see the video?"

"Not at all. Pops, would you mind showing this officer the surveillance video?" Melodie asked.

"Sure thing. As long as the Bitch goes outside first. I'm tired of her stench smelling up my house." Digger replied.

"You can't kick me out of here, old man." Annie sneered.

"Oh?" Digger asked. "Bitch, I can kick you out, I can push you out, Hell I can even personally throw you out! I ain't so old I can't lift your scrawny ass off the ground! I just don't want to dirty my hands with your shit covered clothes. Now get out of my house before you eat a size thirteen!"

"Are you going to let him threaten me like this?" Annie demanded.

"Unless he attempts to put a hand on you, there's not much we can do. This is his home. If he doesn't want you inside, we have to abide by his wishes."

Before Annie could make her way outside, Marla came downstairs, holding tightly to the handrail.

"What is going on?" Marla asked softly, drawing everyone's attention.

"Marla!" Annie cried, trying to run over to her.

"Don't come near me!" Marla shouted.

"Baby! How did you get here?!" Annie asked, trying to play the part of a concerned parent.

"Like you even give a shit," Marla said.

"How can you say that?" Annie asked. "Of course, I care."

"You care about the paychecks you're going to stop getting."

"What? Who said anything about paychecks? Baby, there are no paychecks. Someone is filling your head with lies."

"You mean my Dad wasn't worth over three-hundred million dollars? Or that you were getting a monthly check to take care of me? Or , the fact I never saw a cent, as long as I was with you? No new clothes, no warm jackets, no bed, nothing. I slept on a mattress, on the floor. And I wasn't allowed to eat the food in the trailer. It belonged to your family. I either ate at school or Stella and Spence's place, but God help me if I ever tried to eat at the fucking trailer."

Annie glared at Marla before she let a few tears leak from her eyes.

"I don't know why you're letting these people fill your head with all sorts of lies," Annie sniffed. "But I don't like it, and it needs to stop."

"I don't give a fuck what you like." Marla snapped.

"I never liked how you treated your children or me. But then we all have to deal with what we don't like, right?"

"Your behavior needs to change, right now!" Annie snapped.

"Or what?" Marla asked. "You're going to send me away? You keep threatening to. Didn't Chuck finally sell me to the highest bidder, just like he threatened to? I have a receipt showing the contract, with both of your signatures, so you must know something about it."

Annie's eyes widened with fear. And when one of the Police Officers asked what Marla was speaking about, Annie tried to blow it off as a joke.

Opening up her backpack, Marla pulled out several thick pieces of paper, rolled up, and tied them together. Anyone looking could see where someone cut open an official wax seal very carefully. They wanted it left intact, so whoever looked at it could see who the seal belonged to.

"But I have the contract right here," Marla said. "It has everyone's signature on it. It says you and Chuck sold me for two million dollars. But guess what? I don't give a fuck how much you sold me for. You can tell Salvatore he can kiss my ass. I'm not going with him. Ever."

Before Annie could reply, a heavily accented voice spoke from the doorway. Two men wearing three-piece suits stood watching the drama unfold as if they didn't have a care in the world.

"Oh, ragazza mia, verrai con me. E molto prima di quanto pensi. Soprattutto se non vuoi che accada nulla a questi delinquenti che chiami amici e familiari. Avrò i miei uomini qui nelle prossime ore se non parti con me, e nessuno di loro sarà lasciato vivo. La loro morte sarà sulle tue spalle. (Oh, my girl, you will be coming with me. And much sooner than you think. Especially if you don't want anything to happen to these delinquents you call friends and family. I will have my men here within the next few hours if you don't leave here with me, and not one of them will be left alive. Their deaths will be on your shoulders.)

Melodie and Axel both walked behind Marla and put a hand on her shoulders. It didn't matter if they understood what the man in the fancy suite said to her, the threat was clear, and she had their support.

"Do not give in to whatever he said to you. We'll get through this, I promise." Melodie told her daughter.

"Sembra che le tue minacce non spaventino la mia nuova famiglia. Quindi, hai la mia risposta. Preferirei morire con la mia famiglia che andare ovunque con un pezzo di merda come te o uno dei tuoi soci. (It seems your threats do not scare my new family. So, you have my answer. I would rather die with my family than go anywhere with a piece of shit like you or any of your ass ociates.) Marla replied, angering the man in the suit.

"You have just made the worse decision you could, Marla, for everyone." The man snarled.

"Really, Salvatore?" Marla asked, feigning sweetness. "How could I do that?"

"You just signed everyone's death note."

"You forget which country we're in, Sal."

"It does not matter! I own every country!" Salvatore shouted.

"Not this country. And here I'll see you in Hell before I go anywhere with you."

"You will regret trying to fuck with me, little girl."

With that, Sal grabbed Annie by the back of her shirt before she could do anything. Keeping her in front of him, Sal pushed Annie out of the house and over to his car.

"Get in!" He snarled.

"Hey!" She cried.

"Now, before I get angrier!"

"Fine!" Annie huffed but didn't say another word.

Back inside the house, the Police Officers looked over the papers Marla had handed them while Marla was looking at Axel and Melodie.

"He's going to come back with his men to kill everyone." She told them.

"Let him try," Axel said. "We'll be ready. Besides, we have some help of our own on the way."

Jack spoke up from the phone. "Are you Marla?"

"No, Sir. I'm Marcie." Melodie gasped upon hearing the name. "Marla's the name those bastards gave me. I'm going back to the name my Mom gave me when I was born."

"Good for you, Marcie, but to answer your question, I'm Jack. I'm part of a special military unit that has been tracking Salvatore and Timon for years. We could never pinpoint where the Bastard is, though. Every time we found him, he went back underground. Now, we know exactly where he's going to be. And we're going to be there to capture the son-of-a-bitch."

"Okay," Marcie said, "But I have to ask why. Why are you so interested now?"

Spence practically answered her with one question of his own when he spoke up.

"Uncle Jack?"

"Hey, Bud. You hang in there. Uncle Tate and I are coming to get you and Stella. I promise." Jack told him, then spoke to Marla again.

"Because Marcie, Salvatore just threatened a place where our niece and nephew are. He threatened to kill every person in the home, including them. No one, especially a sick human trafficking Mobster, threatens our family and lives to tell about it."

AFTERWARD

I hope everyone enjoyed my first novella, Going Through Hell: Inferno Wolves. This novella is the prequel to the Covert Ops Trilogy that I have been trying to figure out for a long time, and now it seems I am finally starting to make it happen!

I want to thank Rosie Quintana, Mrs. Petermeier, and my Mom for always telling me I will succeed in my writing if I keep trying and not give up. Without the three of you, I would not have the strength to pursue my dreams. And Mrs. Petermeier, I'm sorry the people I named after you in this book were such villains! I know it's not the same as me signing a book for you, but I was more than half-asleep when I first named the characters, and when I saw which characters I named after you, I wasn't going back through to rename them. Sorry!! You are still my favorite teacher, though, and I will always love you!! I also want to thank Cheryl Demont. You have been a lifesaver, going over my story, giving me your opinions, and helping me think of alternative ideas when something doesn't sound quite right. And your sense of humor has gotten me through a few killer nights!! Thank you so very much!

So, for those who have just finished Going Through Hell, I am already working on the trilogy's first book.

Unlike the fantastic T.S. Joyce or the phenomenal Elle Boone, I will not be able to pop a book out every month, unfortunately. Maybe one day I'll become as outstanding as they are, but alas, that day has not arrived. So until then, I'm hoping to release the first book of the trilogy in two to three months with everything going on. And if everything works out, who knows, maybe it could turn out to be longer than a trilogy since I have more story ideas.

If you want to reach out to me, though, I always look forward to hearing from my readers. You can reach me at kymkjoneswriting@gmail.com .

Kymber Jones

www.ingramcontent.com/pod-product-compliance
Lightning Source LLC
LaVergne TN
LVHW050419160726
843469LV00041B/1142

* 9 7 8 9 3 5 4 5 8 0 3 6 9 *